The Price of Being Young

Diana Castaños

The Price of Being Young

Translated by
William Bainbridge

© Diana Castaños, 2019
© Bokeh, 2019

Translated by William Bainbridge

Leiden, NEDERLAND
www.bokehpress.com

ISBN 978-94-93156-04-3

To Emilio Castaños, because we are what we love

I

Before doing the magic

My name is Josefina, but everyone calls me Jo.

It's not that they want to call me Jo. Actually, they don't care about it at all. What happens is that I always manage to get what I want. For example, I give them such a tantrum that they think twice before calling me Josefina again.

Anyways, be patient with me, because I'm not used to telling stories. It's just that normally nothing happens in my life. Since I was a child I've kept diaries, but although I entertain myself while I write them, the truth is that I can barely fill them. Luckily, these last weeks have been very exciting, and I have things to tell.

Where to begin? Ah, yes… I have to go back to a month ago, at the beginning of the holidays. And I also have to explain some things.

The house where I live is old, but very big. That doesn't matter, though, because my sister, my mother and I have to sleep cramped in a single room, on the first floor, while the rest of the rooms are full of junk. My father used to live here too, but one day he got tired of it being so confined. Or maybe he got tired of other things. Here there are many things to be tired of.

On the ground floor of the house lives my grandmother, always reminding us that the house belongs to her and that she is the one that allows us to stay; and my great-grandmother, Granny Trina, who cooks Spanish sweets, and often speaks in enigmas.

You may have noticed that Josefina is an old woman's name. It's like that because when my grandmother, who's the one that decided my name, named me, wasn't thinking about me, but about my great-great-grandmother, who was born in Spain at the beginning of the 20th century (apparently in that time the name was quite fashionable).

My grandmother is like that. She decides for someone, years before that person even begins to consider the matter. She determines what vases are placed on what table, whether we leave the house or not, if the glasses in the room are well polished, what I will do during my vacation time… and on and on. For example, she decided that this year I will spend the summer studying. As if I was not bored enough at school, I have to endure teachers all of July and August.

As I have the worst grades in my class, my grandmother thinks that if they do not give me private tutors, I'll be stupid. My sister says that whatever they do, I have no choice, that I'll stay like this anyway. I agree with her. I am not interested in cultivating myself; sometimes I would rather burn my soul before learning something.

Today, for example, my piano teacher Tania came. I hid under the bed. They dragged me out. Then, I went out and sat down at the piano. Tania was serious; the mouth in a perfect straight line. She asked me to play in C major. I asked her to let me go to the bathroom. I went to the kitchen, turned on the gas, and lit a match. Everyone was alarmed! What a big deal they made for just a match.

They scolded me viciously and sent me to my room. I was the happiest girl! My piano lesson was finished.

My great-grandmother stuck her head in the room. She always manages to be present everywhere.

–You can lead a horse to water, but you can't make him drink –she said, mysteriously.

Maybe the story that I just told seems very interesting, but it's only one of the few things that happened this summer. Actually, life in the house is usually very boring; you can even hear the sound of a fly. My mom says it's because we appreciate silence. But my sister and I believe that it's not peace, but fear of our grandmother. The only interesting thing that happens here has to do with what I create.

I'm often so bored that I invent a story in my head. I'm grateful for my imagination. It saves me. When my Spanish teacher, that my grandmother chose, sends me to write, he must also order me to stop writing, because I invent things so funny that it's hard for me to drop my pencil and return to real life.

Sometimes I complain to Boni, my sister, the only one who ever listens to me even a little bit in the house these days. I tell her that my soul is about to go live in another body, from so much boredom that Chi has in mine. She usually replies that I'm a little girl and that I don't understand anything.

My sister Boni is named after Bonifacia, the sister of Granny Trina. Boni isn't worried about my boredom. The problem with her is that all she wants in life is for people to leave her alone. Unfortunately, that doesn't happen when you live in the same house as our grandmother.

Boni also has private tutors this summer. She doesn't need them, because she is the smartest person in her class (teachers never believe I'm her sister), but Grandma doesn't want her to waste time. Boni just wants to listen to music, and leave the house, but my grandmother would burn the city before allowing one of us out of her sight during the summer.

Of course, Boni protested when she was banned from leaving.

–I'm not Jo! I'm not a little girl! Why can't I leave? –she shouted at the top of her lungs.

–I consider that you have a lot to learn –determined our grandmother.

–Mom! –Boni called out uncontrollably.

Mom came into the room. Her eyes were tired, and you could see that the yelling had given her a headache.

–I'm tired of all of you. I want everyone to move out of my house! –my grandmother declared.

My mother flared her nose and her eyes got big like doll sleeves. My grandmother knew that she had said too much, and she remained immobile; even her threatening hands stopped in the middle of the air, without finishing the gesture. It seemed that she was afraid of her own words, as if she regretted saying them.

–Then, we will go! –Boni shouted.

–Quiet, Boni! –my mother ordered.

There is no one who understands my mother. She can yell at Grandma, but if Boni or I do, it's a problem.

–Right now, to your room, Boni! –she ordered.

Boni gave my mother a laser-beam look, but she turned around and left. My mother continued to argue with Grandma. If I could write about these arguments each time the Spanish teacher asked me to write something, a while ago I would have written a thousand paragraphs. But it's definitely not allowed.

II

I left my mom and grandmother to argue and slipped away to see my sister. Boni was lying face up on the bed, she had her headphones on and was trying to dive into her music; but you could clearly see that she was very upset and that her mood wouldn't allow her to.

I touched her.

—Leave me alone! —she roared, as if she was going to eat me.

I hate when she gets upset with me for something that I didn't do.

—I came to help you.

—I don't need your help. You're a toddler! You don't understand anything.

My sister is two years older than me, but she acts as if she were twenty.

—You're just like Mom! —I snapped.

Oddly enough, that interested her.

—How is that? —Boni asked, leaving her headphones to the side.

—Even when it seems Mom is on your side; she ends up shouting at you.

—Mom behaves like that because, though she knows I'm right, she can't avoid being the way she is —Boni explained.

How could she defend her like that! I don't get it. Mom had just fought with her and then she took Mom's side!

—I'm glad you're named Bonifacia!

Boni lit up. There is nothing that bothers her more than to shout her full name.

–Oh, Josefina, now you're going to get it… –Boni threatened me and left the room.

Poor Boni. It must be difficult to have that name. It's worse than mine.

However, my sister didn't inspire any pity when she returned to our bedroom. She reappeared with a smile that disturbed me. It wasn't good when she had that smile.

–Look what I have here! –taunted Boni.

It was my crystal collection.

I've met kids who collect stamps and coins, and children who collect dead butterflies (a little sick, don't you think?). Norah, my best friend, and also a neighbor of ours, collects books (which I think is boring).

I like to collect colorful crystals. They are beautiful, and unique, and if you put them in the sun, they shine as if they were alive. My grandmother hates them, which increases my love for the collection. She says I look like a fool when I begin to look at them, and she threw all of them away that I didn't hide in the window sill. What I couldn't imagine is that Boni knew where my hiding place was.

–I'm taking these dirty crystals to Grandma and she's going to throw all of them in the trash.

It looked like Boni wasn't kidding. I began to tremble.

I imagined what my grandmother would tell me:

–You're leaving this house right now, Jo! And never come back!

I imagined myself packing. I would pack my blanket, to go sleep under a bridge, and my knife, to slice the food I would find on the street. I would take my journal with me, to narrate my sorrows, and my colorful crystals, to put them in the sun, so they could shine. I would see how beautiful they were, and I would think about the house, and I would miss my mom, and even Boni. I visualized everything so clearly that tears began to fall on my face. I was crying, like a flowing river. I imagined that one day, by pure coincidence, I would meet my grandmother. She would walk out of the hairdresser and I would be under a bridge looking at my crystals. Then, she would approach me with tears in her eyes and would ask me to return home. But I would look at her with indifference and I would ask: «Who are you, ma'am?» Then, she would, drowning in sorrow, say...

But I didn't have time to think about what she would say, because my mom came into the room and jumped on Boni.

–Why do you bother your sister? Can't you see she's crying?

–I haven't done anything –Boni defended–. She began to cry herself.

–Give me that! –I snatched my crystals and, without knowing why, dropped them on the floor.

Regretfully, I bent down to pick them up, but then I saw that the most beautiful ones were the most broken. I felt anger building in me; the worst of rages, the one against oneself. I picked up the ones that remained intact, and I threw them back against the ground. My mother and Boni watched as I crushed them on the floor, again and again, but they didn't interrupt me.

When I finished, my mother embraced me with love and she pressed my head against her chest. Then, she spoke to Boni without looking at her. You could see she was blaming herself for my tantrum.

–Collect the crystals and remove them. Then, go back to your room and do not leave until tomorrow. Understood?

–Yes –Boni agreed.

We left the room. I had my head against Mom's chest.

III.

While we were going down the stairs, Mom brushed the hair out of my face.

–Jo, I've neglected you.

She seemed worried.

–I haven't paid much attention to you lately –more than with me, she was talking to herself.

I hugged her tightly. I felt that she needed it. Older people never accept it, but they need a lot of affection from their children. She returned the hug and in my ear she told me, softly:

–I just spoke with your Spanish teacher.

I felt a surge of danger nearby.

–By phone?

–No; he is downstairs.

–In the house?

–Yes.

–What is he here for? I don't have class today!

–He came to talk with me.

That intrigued me. What did Brick Head want to say to my mother?

Actually, my teacher isn't named Brick Head, but I call him that, as revenge. Most of all because he likes dictations so much. And when he dictates, I get bored. For instance, he says: «The flowery fields that exist in the south of Cuba...» And I write: «Poppies, gladioli, lilies, sunflowers and the hydrangeas of Cuba...»

Then he approaches to me and looks at it.

–But, Jo! What is that? That's not what I dictated! What do you have in your head? Bricks?

–But, Mr. Professor –my grandmother forces me to say «Mr. Professor» to Brick Head–, I'm not guilty of that. When you say «flowery fields» I immediately begin to imagine poppies, gladioli, lilies, sunflowers… and that's what I write. It's not my fault. It's my imagination's fault.

Or when he dictated: «When Christopher Columbus arrived for the first time, Cuba was inhabited by the *Siboneyes* and the *Taínos*, who spoke in the Arawak language…», I wrote: «The aborigines who were living in Cuba became extinct because of the exploitation they suffered from the Spaniards, and also because of the diseases that the Spaniards brought with them. The *Siboneyes* and the *Taínos*, who spoke the Arawak language, are already extinct in Cuba…»

When Brick Head sees what I'm writing, he removes the pencil from my hand.

–But, Jo! What is that? That's not what I dictated!

–But, Mr. Professor, it's not my fault. You are not giving all the information, and I, since I know it, write it down. It's not my fault. I have a lot of knowledge about the subject.

–I give up! I can't put up with this girl! Bricks, bricks are what you have in your head!

My great-grandmother, who always listens to everything, and moves stealthily throughout the house, supported me with a phrase that she said is from Goethe: «In the works of man, the worthiest of attention is the intention». However, it didn't help much: Brick Head ignored her. I think he hardly even noticed her; he was too horrified of me.

Precisely because of this story I've shared, it didn't look good to me that Brick Head had come to talk to my mother. And I liked it even less when my mother informed me:

–And he wants to talk to you, too.

No, that definitely didn't sound good.

Mom gently guided me to the living room. There was Brick Head waiting for us. He gave me a look of pity that left me very intrigued. Granny Trina poked her head inside of the room, just as she usually does, and declared:

—Intention creates guilt and crime.

But I didn't know what she was talking about. I had no intention of anything. I was waiting, without any intention. And Brick Head didn't seem to have any purpose either. He was drinking tea, very absorbed, as if he were alone in the living room. He didn't seem interested in talking. In fact, he sipped his tea so slowly that I almost grew old between the sips. Suddenly, I started to have a huge curiosity about what was happening outside the window.

Beyond the garden of the house, you could see the neighbors. They had returned from their trip to England. Norah, my best friend, had promised me that she would bring me a gift. She even asked, in front of me, money from her father to buy something for me. I immediately wanted the scene with Brick Head to end quickly. But he didn't seem to have even an ounce of hurry. He began:

—Jo, I want to apologize if I've ever been hard on you.

—What?

If it hadn't been so slow, it might have been a lot more interesting to have an adult apologize to me.

—Sometimes older people make mistakes...

Sometimes? More like every minute. But I didn't want to stop him, I needed him to finish talking so I could escape and go see Norah. She's a couple of years older than me, just like my sister, but she doesn't act cocky about it. Quite the opposite. She explains a lot of things to me, and knows how to recognize when I surpass her knowledge of something.

But Brick Head seemed to have intentions to delay the meeting forever. I had to hurry it. I put on an angel's face and said:

–What's this about, Mr. Professor?

Brick Head stopped. He opened his eyes a little and he nodded.

–You're right. I'll go straight to the point.

He handed me my notebook from our class.

–Look what you have written about your family.

I didn't have to look at my text. I had written it, so I knew what it said. But my mother took the notebook.

–Look, darling, read it. Don't you think there's something strange?

The text read:

MY FAMILY

My Dad is a great person. His only defect is that he cannot stand to live in this house; and that's why my Dad has moved out. Wherever my Dad has gone, I know he will be fine. I'm not concerned where he may be, but that he returns someday. This house is more fun when he is around. For example, Dad doesn't scold me for keeping raisins under the tablecloth, or because I break another glass. I know he would have understood when I threw the hamster into the toilet (it was an accident). He would have understood because my Dad is a great person. But he is the only one that is amazing here.

Jo

I didn't believe there was anything wrong with my text. It was the pure, hard truth. But Brick Head pointed out what was wrong.

–It was a composition about the family, and you only spoke about your dad.

So that was it.

–My daughter! She's so stressed!

My mother burst into tears. Sometimes, my mother can really be an actress. She began crying so loud! I saw that Norah had closed the window of her room. There was almost half a block in between, and she still heard my Mom crying.

They had asked me for a composition about my family, and my Dad was a member of it. Nobody mentioned that I had to talk about ALL the members of my family. Adults sometimes make a fuss out of nothing.

—Can I leave? —I asked, closing the matter.

—Sure, my darling, go rest —my mother stammered. She was covered in tears. Her face had turned red and was full of snot, which she tried to disguise.

Brick Head gave her a handkerchief.

—My daughter is so fragile —Mom cried.

I took advantage of Mom being the center of attention and I left.

—A stitch in time saves nine —said Granny Trina when she saw me sneak away, but I didn't know if she was referring to Brick Head, Mom, or me.

—Goethe? —I asked.

—Victor Hugo —she answered, with eyes glazed over.

IV.

–Why did your mom and dad break up? –Norah wanted
to know.

–Because of Mariela.

–Another woman, huh?

–No, my father isn't one of those. Mariela is my grandmother.

–Ah –Norah was curious. She hesitated before daring to
ask–. And why is your grandmother to blame for the breakup?

–My grandmother used to remind him every single day that
the house we live in wasn't his, and would ask him to move out.

–And your dad endured that?

–Yes. For us.

–It's hard to be a man and put up with that.

–That's hard no matter what gender you have!

–Yes, yes, of course. But for men it's even more difficult. I
live with my dad, and I know: they need to believe they are
stronger than anyone.

–My father isn't one of those, either.

Norah wanted to change the subject.

–And where's your dad now? –she wondered.

–I don't know... he doesn't even call me...

–I already know what happens in your house! Your grandmother is a monarch!

–She isn't that.

–I just came from England –Norah explained–. I know what
I'm saying. Do you know what a monarch is?

–Something like a dictator?

–It's someone who commands all the people around them. All the time. Forever.

–Forever?

I began to think about how long forever is.

–Do you know what can be done to a monarch?

–What?

–An overthrow of state –she announced, very sure of herself.

–How's that?

–People take control by force.

What a great idea! I could overthrow the State of Grandma! I would go and say: «From now on, I'm the one that makes the commands!» How is it, that I had never tried it? I would allow her to live in the house, because she was too old to leave, but it would be under my rules.

Then, I imagined my rules:

Jo's RULES

–Boni and I will each have our own room, and mine will be full of crystals.

–It is obligatory that my Dad lives with us.

Norah was so smart! I thanked her for giving me the idea; but she laughed.

–You cannot give your grandmother an overthrow of state.

–Why not?

–Because you're not strong. To overthrow a monarch, you have to be strong. Can you imagine giving your Grandma a command and her slapping you and sending you to your room as a punishment?

Yes, I could imagine that.

Then, Norah began explaining to me why it's difficult to remove a monarch.

–… for example, in England, it's not easy to remove the Queen. Because even if she doesn't work or contribute to the economy, Royalty has existed for so many years, that the people are already accustomed to it.

The same is true with my Grandma, I thought: she has been commanding my mother, Boni and me for so many years that we already believe it's normal. But it is not normal.

In that moment, Mr. Hamze, Norah's father, arrived.

–Good afternoon, Miss Jo –he greeted me.

–Mr. Hamze, do you want to overthrow the state of my grandmother?

Norah started to laugh in such an intense way that she fell backwards.

–I do not want anything to do with your grandmother, Miss.

–Why not?

Mr. Hamze is a diplomat, he has spent a lot of time living in England, and he always behaves like such a square. Therefore, I had to ask him in an explicit way:

–I don't want a diplomatic response. I want the truth. The raw truth.

–My father can't speak candidly even if he really tries. It's not in his blood –Norah said, softly.

But Mr. Hamze seemed to feel good about the challenge.

–If you allow me to say it, Miss, I will tell you the truth as you ask for it.

–I'll let you.

Mr. Hamze sat down and leaned forward.

–There are two types of neighbors in this world –he began–: Those who make your life more pleasant, and those who do not.

It was clear what type my grandmother was. What I didn't understand was how a nice neighbor behaved. I asked him.

–Well, a long time ago… when none of you were born… in fact, when I was still a child… I used to live in this same house, and except for your grandmother's place, Miss, there was nothing around here. Nothing at all. All this was quite desolate.

–No cafés, no schools, no cinemas…?

–None of that. There were only houses, and only a few.

Suddenly, Mr. Hamze's face loosened up. He actually began to show a tender expression, and it was as if he was reborn under his skin. He leaned forward, and told me a story that left me both fascinated and upset at the same time.

–«In one of those houses, one which was far away, lived an old man».

«He was a very sullen man. The house was made of wood, and it was right in front of the beach. A few meters from the water, he had succeeded in, I do not know how, growing vegetables, especially bananas. And he had a scarecrow, one so big and real, that it seemed more alive than the man himself».

«This man was engaged with the scarecrow more than with the garden itself: Every day he changed its clothes and its hat. He talked to it, he sang songs to it, he lulled it on stormy days».

«I, who saw him every day from my window, began to respect that man, who did not talk to anyone, but who sang to his scarecrow. I wanted to show my appreciation, but I could not find a correct way, because the man was very sullen, and whenever I got close, he dodged me. I did not want to change him: I liked how he was; I just wanted to show him my respect».

«One day, I looked for the hat that my father had given me for my birthday. It was a black leather hat, very expensive, but I've always believed that the things we give to others must be important things to us, otherwise the act doesn't have any meaning. Then, I took the hat and put it at the feet of the scarecrow, without the man noticing me».

«He did not see me, but he knew it was me. I cannot explain how. He knew it, as I guessed he would put something for me in the same place. The next day I looked at the feet of the scarecrow. There were candies and some books. Somehow, the man knew that I liked to read».

«That's how we behaved for several years. We never talked to each other, but I used to put at the feet of the scarecrow what I thought would please the old man, and he almost always left me books, and candies».

«One day I needed to go to England, to study at the University. I wanted to say goodbye to the old man, to see him and thank him for the books he had given me for so many years, but that would have been breaking our agreement of silence. It would have been like violating the magic. We were friends without talking to one another. We were like invisible guardians for each other».

«I went to a plant store and bought, with the little money I had at the time, seeds of poppies and sunflowers. I thought they would give color to the old man's house. I put them in the pocket of the scarecrow, along with a postcard that had the address of the place I would be living in England. It was my way of saying goodbye».

«Years later, while living in England, almost about to graduate, I received a postcard. Nothing was written, but it had the address of the old man's house; and I had a bad feeling. I, who had not come for several vacations, decided to take the time to go visit him. When I arrived, he was gone. He had died. And your grandmother, who never liked the old man because of how reclusive he was, had sent someone to destroy the scarecrow».

«She had not, however, commanded that the poppies and sunflowers next to his house be cut down».

Mr. Hamze leaned back.

«And that's it».

He put his hands on his knees, and stayed like that for a moment.

—Is the house still there?

–There is something left... not much –he said, but it didn't look he was talking to me.

–And the flowers? The sunflowers and the poppies?

–Without care, they died. When I finally returned from studying in England, they weren't there anymore.

Mr. Hamze slowly got up. He remained standing in the middle of the room for a while. Norah was quietly looking at him. Little by little, his face was leaving the tenderness aside, until he completely recovered his usual, tight face. He turned around and closed the door behind him. We remained in silence. A deep and compact one, that took us a while to depart.

When I finally spoke, I felt ashamed, without knowing why.

–Norah, did you know that story?

–Some parts, but not completely. My father changed that day... or at least that's what he says.

–How did he change?

–I don't know. He hasn't ever explained it to me. But I do know that the death of the old man was hard for him.

I remained silent. It bothered me that the old man had died. But I was also feeling uncomfortable with another thing. It took me a while to realize what it was. When I finally did, I tried to remedy it.

–Norah, what if we buy seeds of magnificent flowers? We can plant them where the old man had his.

–You can't even leave your house when you want!

–I can escape when I want!

Norah thought for a moment.

–The best is for you to sow them in your garden. That way you won't have to escape.

It was a good idea. To plant flowers in honor of that weird, good, old man.

–I bet your grandma wouldn't like that idea –said Norah.

I also bet on that. My grandmother doesn't believe in quiet people. She sees it as a sign of a lack of education. The truth is that I wasn't like the old man in that way. I can't keep my mouth shut for more than five minutes. But the story of Norah's father had found a place in my soul, and in that moment, I admired the silence.

–Norah, give me my gift; I'm leaving. I want to be in silence.

–What gift?

–You told me you were going to bring me a gift from England.

Norah put her hands on her head.

–I forgot it!

I started kicking the floor.

–How are you going to forget my gift!

–Wait! Wait! I brought these English books. Do you want to read them?

–Did you spend the money for my gift on some books?

–They're so good! –Norah sighed.

–Well, if they are that good, they better stay with you!

I opened the window of the room, grabbed the windowsill with both hands and jumped out of the house. At the front door of Norah's house was Mr. Hamze, smoking a cigar. His face was stretched as usual, as he took long puffs of his cigar. (My grandmother hated him for that habit, more than for any other thing).

–Could you, Miss, not use the window for leaving our house? –he asked me.

–Well, no. «Miss» can't do that! Just like your «Miss Daughter» can't keep a promise!

Mr. Hamze had taken a puff of his cigar, and my answer left him so surprised that he forgot to blow out the smoke. It came out through his nose and mouth. He coughed a little.

—Smoking is an ugly habit —I spit out, turned my back, and went home. Or maybe, I should say, to my grandmother's house, where I live.

V.

When I arrived at the house, Grandma was complaining about the rats. Lately it's her favorite subject.

–They live in the basement!

–There aren't any rats there! –rippled my mother.

–I listen to them all the time –Grandma insisted.

–You are imagining things –my mother repeated over and over again.

–I'm not crazy yet, Magdalena. Remember, this is my house and I know all the sounds.

–I know very well that this is your house, Mom. You won't allow me to forget it.

–Then, you also know that what I say is true: you three live on the first floor; your grandmother and I live down here on the ground floor, and... do you know who lives in the basement?

–I do not.

My grandmother looked at her as if my mother was abnormal.

–The rats!

It's true that sometimes you hear noises in the basement. But I had never thought about that. Maybe my grandmother was right (although I would never tell her).

I took advantage of their disagreement and went quietly to my room, before my grandmother saw me and sent me to clean the dust off the furniture, or some other nonsense. However, the floorboards in the house are old, and they squeaked under my feet.

–That's how I wanted to catch you.

–Hi, Grandma –I said, feigning innocence.

That put her on guard.

–Come here, Jo!

–I can't right now, Grandma, I have to go to the toilet.

–Go then, but after that, I want you to come down here, you have to clean the furniture in this room.

My mother came in my defense:

–But, Mom, didn't I tell you what happened with the Spanish professor?

–Do not «Mom» me, Magdalena. Don't be fooled by the clever bug that you have as a daughter. She is perfectly fine; she is deceiving you and all of us. What I have just said, Jo! You go to the bathroom and come right back; there are things to clean in here…

–Yes, Grandma. You have my word.

On the stairs was my great-grandmother.

–Hi, Granny Trina. Did you hear Grandma: Jo, do this; Jo, do that. Do you think someday I'll have peace in this house?

–There can be no pact between the lion and the man, just as the wolf and the donkey cannot live in harmony –she said.

I regretted asking. Actually, it was a rhetorical question.

Boni was there in our room:

–Jo, forgive me.

She extended her hands. She had my colorful crystals. She had taken the job of putting them back together with super glue.

–Did Mom tell you about the Brick Head letter?

–Yes.

–Did that make you feel pity for me?

–No, it's not that…

But I knew it was. I know Boni. She usually feels really bad after treating me like a child. But I didn't care if she recognized it or not. I didn't even pay attention to the crystals. Glued together, they didn't have any beauty, and I preferred not to look at them. In addition, I had other things in my head. I started to rummage through the drawers.

–What are you looking for? –Boni was very kind. And to say she wasn't experiencing sorrow for me!

–I'm looking for my diary from last year –I answered.

–What period?

I hate when she plays dumb.

–What period will it be? Our last vacation!

She looked worried, but for real, she wasn't pretending anymore. She helped me search.

In the end we found it under my dirty socks, in the basket of clothes to be washed.

–What is your diary doing here? –Boni asked, but then she made a gesture in the air, like shooing an answer away.

I searched through my journal for the pages I wanted to read. Norah had asked me why Mom and Dad had separated. That question had left me thinking. I opened my diary. I knew exactly what page to read.

FRAGMENTS OF MY VACATION DIARY FROM THE PREVIOUS YEAR

Tuesday, July 5th

We were at the table, eating a Catalan cream, a Spanish dessert that Granny Trina, who practically lives in the kitchen, is a specialist at making. This sweet is covered by a thin layer of crunchy caramel, that I especially love to crack.

As we were all busy breaking the top layer with our spoons, we didn't pay any attention to the list my grandmother was completing.

And what a list! It detailed all the things that each of us should do during our holiday. We had just started, and she had already written a whole page. When I finished with my

Catalan cream, I leaned forward to see what assignment she had put under my name. I read something about pulling weeds and painting the fence of the house. It seems that Dad also saw the list, because that was the exact moment when he decided to share, in a casual way, the spark that ignited the fire.

–You know what, Mariela? We're not going to be here for the entire vacation.

I saw the storm approaching. My sister Boni choked on the Catalan cream. Her dry cough was the only thing that could be heard in the environment for a few minutes, but nobody paid any attention to her.

–Who is «we», Daniel? –inquired my grandmother, pushing the tip of the pencil into the paper, just below the assignments under Dad's name–. Who are the ones that won't be here for all of the holidays?

–We: Magdalena, Boni, Jo, and I. We're going on vacation for fifteen days to Russia. Well, the girls will be on vacation. I have to work. But I'll be with them as much as I can…

My grandmother interrupted him, bluntly, like someone who crushes a fly against the wall.

–Over my dead body!

–We'll see.

–Magdalena –my Grandma spoke to my mother–, what on Earth is your husband telling me?

–Nothing, Mom, nothing…

My Dad got very upset. He always gets upset when my Mom doesn't stand up for herself or for us in front of my grandmother.

–Magdalena, tell Mariela what we've talked about –my father said.

But my mother was speechless.

–It's better not to; let's leave the topic, Daniel. It's not the right time –she whispered.

–When is the right time, Magdalena? –my father got upset–. I'll say it once more: you are the one that allows your mother to take charge of our lives.

–Daniel, no…

–The girls are growing up in this environment because you permit this to happen, Magdalena –my father went on and on.

Mom flared her nose. Her eyes widened, like doll sleeves, and she turned directly to my father. She exploded:

–Now it's my fault! Everything is my fault! I am the one who wanted to go live in any small apartment, but not you; you need to wait until you buy the house of your dreams.

–If you demand respect, we can live in this house!

My grandmother decided to interrupt:

–What pot of crickets is this? If you are going to have a fight, you need to go to your room; here, we are eating.

My parents instantly got quiet.

–Well, now, I'm going to read the list of things that everyone has to do this summer –my grandmother continued, as if nothing had happened.

–Give them an inch and they'll take a mile –commented Granny Trina.

My grandmother ignored her and started reading the list.

The Catalan cream lost its flavor inside my mouth, but I kept myself from making even the smallest comment.

I read everything out loud. When I finished, Boni's eyes were red. It seemed like she was holding back the urge to cry.

–You don't know everything –she said and got up.

–What are you talking about?

–Look, take this.

She pulled her diary out from under the pillow of her bed. Normally, the only thing she has under her pillow is the book she's reading. I wasn't surprised when she opened to the exact page.

—Read —she prompted me.

WHAT BONI WROTE IN HER DIARY ON JULY 22ND OF LAST YEAR

Friday, July 22nd

It's not that it bothers me that my parents fight. I know that all parents do it. There are some that even do it all the time. Mine do it from time to time. What bothers me is that it's always because of the same reason. I don't understand how it is that they can't resolve it.

Jo thinks they argue because of Grandma. She doesn't understand anything at all. She thinks that Grandma is a bad person and that our parents are the victims. Jo doesn't know that our grandmother is like that because she wants Mom and Dad to be independent and to learn how to figure out life by themselves. Mom also wants Dad to be the kind of man who is able to work really hard so he can hold his head high and not owe anything to anyone. But Dad isn't like that. Dad just wants harmony and peace and things around him to be simple. He doesn't care about hard work at all. He's not willing to sacrifice anything for anybody.

Anyways, they should accept each other as they are, or choose to live separate lives once and for all. They chose the second. What happened at the airport made the situation reach its greatest point of discomfort.

The three of us, Dad, Mom and I, were already at the airport, about to leave for Russia. This was the first vacation where we left the house. The only one that was missing was Jo, who was supposed to arrive with Grandma from an appointment at the dentist. But when Grandma appeared, she was alone.

—Where is Jo? —Mom asked.

—I left her at home, Magdalena. It's a very long trip for such a small girl.

—Mariela, tell me Jo is in the car —threatened Dad.

—You two cannot even take of yourselves as you should, Jo is very small and she needs me —said Grandma—. If I let her go with you, you two may even forget to feed her.

Dad then turned towards Mom.

—Magdalena, say something!

—What do you want me to say, Daniel?

—Tell your mother that what she did is wrong!

—What sense may that have now, Daniel. Let's go to the house.

—What! We are going on our vacation as a family! We are at the airport!

—I won't go to Russia without both of my daughters.

—Here is one of your daughters, who deserves a vacation, and here I am, and I have to go there to work anyways.

—Then, go! I'll stay here with my daughters.

Dad put his hands on his head.

—Whatever! Give me my bags!

Mom gave them to him. He turned his back and left. I kept looking as he walked away, waiting for him to turn and say «Give me my daughter» as he had claimed his suitcases. But he did not.

I returned the journal to Boni.

—Was I the one responsible for Mom and Dad's separation? —I asked with a little voice.

—You weren't the guilty one. You were only the trigger point.

Boni and I would have drowned in our sorrows for a while longer, but someone knocked on the door. It was Mom.

−Jo, go downstairs, you have a visitor.

I went downstairs. Norah was with her father at the door. Mr. Hamze had both hands full; in one he had a little puppy, who subtly whined, and in the other was a paper bag, with what I assumed would be some food for the little animal.

Mr. Hamze asked if he could give me the puppy. He threw the question into the air, looking indistinctly at my grandmother and my mother, but everyone in the room knew it was my grandmother who decided everything in the house. And of course, she didn't like the gift.

−A dog is a sack of fleas. Take that away from here.

Mr. Hamze didn't move. He looked at my mother, asking for support. That was just what was needed. My mother gathered courage and advanced to Mr. Hamze. He extended the puppy and the paper bag. My mother took them while she thanked him for the gift.

Mr. Hamze, tactfully, apologized and left. Norah made some gestures promising we would speak later, but that the moment wasn't good for it. And then they left. Almost running. They knew they had started a storm in our house.

Grandma remained in silence. But she went to her room with a face I had only seen from her a few times and I didn't like it at all.

−Jo, take your puppy and go to your room −my mother asked me, with a trembling voice.

Grandma returned. She had a belt in her hand.

−Mom… −I started to say, but she interrupted me.

−Go, Jo. Now.

I went up to the room with the puppy. All the joy for having it vanished with every blow of Grandma's belt on Mom's back. I hugged the puppy and put myself in the corner of the room.

I looked inside the paper bag: it was a seed. Not a small one, as for a poppy plant. It was a gigantic seed, as big as my hand. I wondered what plant it would be.

–Boni, look at the gifts Norah gave me.

–Ah, good, a dog and a seed.

You could tell by the tone that she was upset with me.

–Why are you angry with me?

–What did you do now? Grandma is beating Mom and it's your fault.

But it wasn't my fault. I don't care what Boni said, everything was Grandma's fault.

Then, a force was born inside of me. I was upset with Boni, who was annoyed with me for every little thing; upset with Mom, who was very weak before my grandmother; upset with the sullen old man, who had died alone; and finally, upset with myself, for letting Grandma make all kinds of decisions for me.

Suddenly, the solution to my problems was clear: I decided to do something against Grandma.

I picked up all the glued crystals that Boni had returned to me. I grabbed the puppy, who still didn't have a name; I found some scissors; and, with the paper bag that contained the seed clenched between my teeth, I climbed through the window, towards the garden.

–What are you doing? –inquired Boni, but I completely ignored her.

It was time to do something to fight Grandma. I didn't have the strength to give her an overthrow of state, but for sure I was able to do black magic, the kind of magic that aborigines in Cuba used to do before they were taught the Christian religion.

The *Siboneyes* and the *Tainos*, who spoke the Arawak language were extinct, but they had left part of their magic in some words.

I sat at the foot of the garden elm and began digging with my hands.

I made two holes. In the first, I sowed the big seed that Norah and her father had given me. In the other, deeper hole, I put my head in, and I sang: «*Guamuaya, guanacabibes, aguacate, mamey...*» and other magic words, that I can't write in here, because they are very dangerous.

When I thought that I had shouted enough in the second hole, I dropped all my crystals inside, glued as they were by Boni. With the scissors, I cut off as much of my hair as I could.

I threw everything into the hole. Then, I looked for the little dog that Norah and her dad had given me. He wasn't anywhere to be found. I had to get up and start calling him. Since he didn't have a name, I had to invent one right then and there. I called him Ps.

Ps still didn't appear. It was as if he could sense that I needed an animal sacrifice to finish the magical ceremony.

In theory, every magical ceremony in Arawak language implies a sacrifice. And the blood sacrifice is quite powerful, but I don't think that it's worth making anyone suffer, so Ps was safe with me. It seems he didn't know that because it took me a long time to find him. Finally, I saw his little tail under the dry fountain of the garden. I grabbed him and cut off some of his hair. It didn't hurt anything, of course.

I put Ps's hair in the hole and covered it well. Then I jumped on top, always repeating «*Guamuaya, guanacabibes, aguacate, mamey...*» and other magic words.

That was it. The magic was already done. My grandmother would suffer in her flesh all of her injustices.

VI

AFTER DOING THE MAGIC

In that moment the doorbell rang. I entered the house running. I saw in a glimpse that my mother, obviously in pain, was zipping her dress. I was glad to have done the magic against my Grandma. I was anxious to know how destiny would make her pay for what she had done.

My mother tried to leave the room. Apparently, she assumed that she was exonerated of being present, maybe because of the severity of her punishment.

But my grandmother didn't see it that way.

–Magdalena, where are you going? Open the door. Can't you hear the bell is ringing? It could be a visitor for you.

My mother went to open the door. It was our mailman. My grandmother receives letters very often, so he treats us with familiarity.

He even displays some pleasantries with Grandma; and he is very kind with Granny Trina, who always offers him her Spanish sweets.

–Hello, Magdalena. How are Mariela and Trina today? –greeted the mailman.

–Do we have a letter? –my Mom asked anxiously, with a trickle of a voice.

–I have two envelopes for you –the mailman was precise. He looked inside the house, looking for my grandmother.

She came out, with a baked apple in her hand, and a blooming smile. No trace of the belt.

–You shouldn't have… –the mailman commented.

—It's not a bother; it's a detail for a gentleman —she said and handed the sweet to him. With the mailman, grandmother always seemed like another person.

The mailman took a bite of the apple.

—It's very tasty!

Granny Trina poked her head out of the kitchen:

—It's a simple dessert; the most important thing is to select the right apple. I prefer them green: it gives a quality of acidity that fits very well with the sweetness of the candy inside.

—When can we try that simple dessert? —I asked.

—After lunch —replied my grandmother sharply.

Granny Trina put her head back into the kitchen. She never got into anything, and avoided problems with Grandma at all costs.

Meanwhile, my grandmother enchantingly watched the mailman, who ate the apple.

—It's good, right? —she didn't stop smiling, nor flattering—. My mother, Trina, learned to cook in Spain, you know…

—Yes, I know that you are from there… from our motherland…

Can you give me the envelopes? —Mom dryly interrupted their flirting, and extended her hand.

Grandma froze her arm with her eyes.

—Magdalena, what manners are those! Excuse me —she spoke to the mailman—, the children of today.

—It's okay, Mariela —he shrugged it off as he handed over the envelopes to Mom—. Sign here, please, Magdalena.

After she signed the mailman's receipt, Mom's hand started to shake. She had noticed that one of the envelopes was a letter from Dad. She held it tight against her chest.

The mailman, who felt the tense atmosphere of the house, said goodbye right away. Grandma started fighting her, but

Mom, atypically, ignored her; she was too absorbed with opening the letter from Dad.

The letter had several pages inside. Mom leafed through them quickly.

She handed one page to Boni and another to me.

–These are for you, from your father –she told us.

–And that other envelope? –Grandma asked Mom.

–Ah... –Mom looked at it quickly–. It has your name on it.

–Give it to me, then! You have your head in the clouds.

Mom extended the envelope to grandmother, without taking her eyes off of Dad's letter.

–He says he's not returning for now, but that he's saving a lot of money... –she gasped with anxiety, her eyes flying through the pages, wanting to devour each line, to read everything at once.

–What did he say? –I asked Boni, who had finished reading her page, which was very short.

–He asked me to have patience with Grandma... and to take care of Mom and you –she summarized.

–He is so far and yet he still manages to make me look like a monster –Grandma was upset.

Boni didn't pay much attention to her. Apparently, she was already putting into practice Dad's advice.

–What did he write to you, Jo? Aren't you going to read it? –wondered Boni.

–Not now. I want to be alone to read it.

Grandma had opened hers. It was a fat envelope, with several papers inside, and some photos of a plump girl.

–Oh, no –Grandma exclaimed, as she began to read the letter.

–What's wrong, Mom? –asked my mother.

–Oh no. I can't. I cannot put up with this!

Granny Trina poked her head back from the kitchen again.

–Grandma is the one who's screaming –I explained.

Then, Granny Trina wiped her hands on her apron, and with a resolute attitude approached the letter. She took it in her hands, leafed through it, and then read it carefully. Grandma had her hands on her head while we waited on pins and needles. Even I forgot about my Dad's letter for a little while.

–In the ailment, patience; in affliction, resignation –recited Granny Trina, when she finished reading the letter.

I had never seen Grandma put her hands on her head, and I was very curious what could have prompted this.

–Oh, Magdalena, as if I didn't have enough already… –complained my grandmother.

–Mom, calm down, what's wrong with you? Give it here, I want to see that letter.

Mom examined the envelope addressed to Grandma. She saw the seals.

–It's from Russia –she reported.

–It's from José –said grandmother.

José is the cousin of Grandma. I had heard his name occasionally; never too much.

Mom held the pages of the letter. It was as long as Dad's letter. Mom read through it, without giving it too much importance:

–He says something about his granddaughter Alina… He says that his granddaughter wants to visit Cuba… Is his granddaughter the girl in this picture?

–The same one. She is a horror of a creature. She has no manners at all –Grandma was distressed–. Her mother herself despised her. My cousin told me about it in other letters.

–Bah, I'm sure it cannot be that bad. Here in the letter –Mom read quickly– he says she speaks Spanish well, but that she doesn't speak very much as a person… And that he expects her to become warmer in the tropics.

44

–What he wants is to get rid of her for a while!

Mom, who continued reading the letter, became excited all of a sudden:

–He says that Daniel was there to visit them! –she murmured some words while she continued reading–. And that he was grateful for their invitation, but he didn't accept accommodation with them.

–So, are we going to receive visitors? –Boni asked.

–Yes. Your cousin from Russia is coming.

–I've never heard of any cousins –Boni objected.

–Her name is Alina. She's the granddaughter of my cousin José. You must attend to her when she comes. She is close to your age –pointed out our grandmother, in an authoritarian tone. You could tell she was already recovering from her anguish.

–But I don't have time to attend to this cousin.

–But you must, and you're going to do it.

–Why?

–Because I say so! –notified Grandma.

–That's not enough! –Boni was annoyed–. There must be more than just commands in this house!

And she ran into our room. Mom followed her, and I followed Mom.

When we entered the bedroom, Boni was lying in her bed, with her headphones on, and she had already taken her favorite position of «I don't care about anything».

–Boni, come here –Mom said softly, while she took out a photo album from the closet–. I want to show you some pictures of our family.

I got closer to see the album, too. Almost all of it was black and white photos, old and boring, but there was also a pretty tree, painted on the album cover.

–What is this drawing, Mom? –I asked.

–That's our family tree. Look, here you are –she put her finger on my name–. See?

–What is that below each name? –I was curious.

–The country and the year in which each person was born. For example, you were born in Cuba, in the year 1996.

–Alina was born in '93, it says here. She is three years older than me.

–We don't know this Alina –interrupted Boni, without taking her headphones off–. Why do we have to attend to her?

–Look, in here there is a picture of her when she was a baby –Mom pointed to a photo of a very white girl, completely bald–. It was sent by your grandmother's cousin years ago…

–To have a picture is not to know someone. Also, she is just a baby there.

–Boni, lie down –my Mom asked, as she placed a pillow behind her back, to make Boni feel more comfortable–. I'm going to tell you a story.

Boni obeyed, but with indifference.

–The mother of José, who as you may know was Bonifacia… –my mother began a story.

–I know that Bonifacia was the sister of Granny Trina! I was named after her –interrupted Boni.

–Yes, indeed. When she and your Granny Trina were young, in the thirties of the last century, a war began in Spain.

–The Spanish Civil War.

–At that time, it still didn't have that name. It was just another war.

–Granny Trina and Bonifacia lived in Spain, but Granny didn't want to stay there in the middle of a war, so she came to Cuba… –I narrated, by memory. Mom had told me that story a few times.

–On the other hand, Bonifacia stayed in Spain –continued Mom from where I had stopped–. Her health wasn't great, she was sick with what she later found out was tuberculosis. She lived with José, who at that time was a child, near a village by the name of Guernica. Trina thought a lot about whether to leave or not, and finally decided that she would emigrate, and she asked her sister to follow her. Bonifacia told her that as soon as her health improved, she would follow her to Cuba.

«But Bonifacia's health never improved. Shortly before the war arrived in Guernica, Bonifacia died. When José became orphaned, he went to the house of a neighbor, whom Bonifacia had asked to take care of him, in case of her death. The neighbor, who was a pleasant and kind-hearted woman, warmly welcomed him. She had the address where Trina had moved to in Cuba, which means, the address of this house; and she decided to write and tell her everything, in order to send José to live with her».

«But, as I said, Spain was at war. The mail hardly worked, and for civilians, even less so. Shortly afterwards, Guernica was razed. The neighbor's letter never arrived. Neither Trina nor your grandmother knew about José for a long time».

«One day, when José was already a man, he wrote to us and told us everything that had happened: how the neighbor had let him live with her and her children; how he grew up and became a man in the middle of the war; and, how he had joined the ranks of the Communist Party of Spain, from which he had to flee, under penalty of death, for the Soviet Union, when the dictatorship began in Spain».

Boni hadn't removed her headphones, but you could see that she was listening carefully, because she had a thin trickle of tears running from her eyes.

–José had a difficult life –Mom continued–. It improved with time, though. In Russia he got married and had a daughter and two grandchildren. One of these grandchildren is Alina, the oldest one, I think. According to what José has told us in other letters, she has serious behavior problems. José is now asking his cousin, that is, your grandmother, to help him. Even if she dislikes the idea of dealing with a spoiled girl, because, as you know, your grandmother doesn't even put up with educated children, she cannot say no to him. Do you understand why?

Boni nodded in silence.

VII.

That same afternoon the preparations for receiving Alina began. Although she was twelve years old and probably wouldn't pay attention to the cleanliness of the house, I witnessed, during Brick Head's lesson, how Mom, Boni and Grandma swept every nook and cranny in the house. I saw spiders, lizards, cockroaches, and even weevils come out: they ran away terrified of the water and soap.

Very soon the house was filled with the horrible smell of bleach, that mixed in the air with the dessert that Granny Trina was preparing in the kitchen, something called *buñuelos al viento*, that according to her caused furor in the Spain of her youth.

–The charm of *buñuelos al viento* is in how light they are from the lack of filling –explained Granny Trina, who, along with me, was the only one exonerated from cleaning the house.

–Does that mean that the *buñuelos al viento* are filled with air? –asked Boni, while cleaning the window.

–If so, then it must be an air with the smell of bleach. I'm not going to eat that –I announced. But I knew that I was going to eat it, and with a lot of pleasure, licking my fingers and everything. Most of all because of the hunger that I had: there is nothing that makes me hungrier than seeing people cleaning.

Granny Trina's sweets, despite being very rich, or maybe precisely because of that, had one drawback: they attracted people. The conditions weren't right for studying: there was movement and disorder all over, buckets of water splashing everywhere, flying rags, scouring pads... Even Brick Head himself didn't listen to his dictations. But the smell of *buñuelos al viento* enveloped him and he extended his class infinitely.

Granny Trina had to offer him a plate of *buñuelos al viento* for him to go away. Once he had tasted them, Brick Head determined that the lessons were finished for the day. I had just closed the door behind him when Grandma came to talk to me.

–Josefina!

–I'm already going to start cleaning! –I thought that was the reason she was calling me–. And it's Jo.

–Jo –she agreed, strangely–. I need your dog.

That didn't sound good.

–What for?

Before Brick Head's class, I had been training Ps. It took me a couple of hours, but I had taught him some good tricks. I had to read a dog training book to do it. Actually, it was very simple. I just had to get Ps to bite a rope and then pull it out of his mouth. Ps was also pulling, and that strengthened his bite. The other thing that I did was tie his legs together, and leave him immobile. After three attempts, he learned to bite the rope and free himself. He had strengthened his bite… and Grandma knew it.

–I want your dog to kill the rats in the basement.

Granny Trina, who heard the conversation, nudged Mom, who was wrapped up in cobwebs, for her to pay attention to our conversation.

–But Ps isn't a cat. He doesn't eat rats.

–But he could bite them, as you taught him to do with the rope. Someone has to put an end to the rats we have in the basement.

–And why Ps?

–Mom, I told you we don't have rats in the basement –said my mother.

—But we do! And that dog lives in my house, like you do, so you have to send it to the basement, Magdalena!

My mother, in a nervous breakdown, grabbed the dog and walked in the direction of the basement. I went after her.

—Mom, no! Don't take him to the basement!

—Jo, go to your room.

—But Mom, Ps isn't ready for that. He's going to be bitten by the rats.

—There are no rats in the basement. Just go to your room —she stopped and stood as tall as she could—. Obey, Jo!

I went to my room. Boni, who had seen everything, came up to the room and tried to comfort me, in her own way.

—Take it, read it —Boni pulled a book out from under her pillow—. It's so good that you're going to forget everything else. It's about a child who discovers that she has powers and... What are you doing?

Boni was startled when she saw me flipping through the pages.

—I read your book.

—You're not reading anything! You are jumping through everything!

—It's boring. The first three pages are for describing the weather.

—What do you have against the weather? —Boni protested.

—Nothing, but it's not necessary to describe it in such detail! I want to skip to the part where the girl displays her powers. It's unacceptable to waste ink describing how much sun there is. The only thing that it explains is that the main character is hot.

—The only unacceptable thing here is you! —Boni declared.

—If I wrote a book, I would make it much more interesting.

—And the part in which the child realizes that she has special powers? Don't you think that's interesting?

—Sure. But that part hasn't arrived yet.

–Of course it has arrived! More precisely, she is the one that is controlling the weather with her powers!

–Where does it say that?

–That's why you have to read the description of how strong the sun is, so you'll realize it's a strange sun, and… Bah, there's no point. I wanted to help you, but you don't understand anything; you're just a toddler.

–I'm not a toddler. I understand well. I just don't want to read a book where, of the many things that could be done with special powers, the person that has them decides to make it hotter.

VIII.

Very soon the house was gleaming, more beautiful than ever. Granny Trina told me that they had also cleaned it like this when I was born, but since I was a baby, I don't remember anything. What a foolish thing: to clean the house for someone who doesn't even have their eyes wide open. Now they could do it for me. I'm already much bigger than a baby and I would notice it.

I wanted to discuss my idea with Boni, but she was upset with me since I discredited her precious book. In addition, she looked quite uncomfortable in our room. We had one extra bed, and hers was now in a corner, which meant that she had less light to read.

The extra bed was for Alina, the cousin who was coming to visit us. Grandma had determined that Alina was going to stay in our room with us. My mother didn't want to oppose her. However, Boni and I dared to protest… in vain.

—The room is pretty small already —I argued to Grandma, while caressing Ps; since Mom had returned him from the basement, Ps didn't leave my side.

—There are six rooms on the top floor, and we have the smallest one —Boni said—. Why?

—Yes, why? —I repeated.

—Because it's my house and in my house, I do what I want —Grandma concluded— and if someone doesn't like it, they are welcome to leave!

No other word was mentioned. That same day, Grandma commanded us to put a single bed that was in one of the empty rooms, into our room. Now our bedroom looked really tight; we barely had space to walk.

—There isn't any space —I snapped at Grandma, when she came to see her work.

—That's because the dog is here. You have to send him to the basement again.

—He's not leaving! —I cried, as I pressed him against me.

—Of course he's leaving! Also, I need him to take care of the rats.

—Mom already took him down there!

—But it didn't help. I keep hearing noises. So, he has to live in the basement from now on.

—Cats are the ones that eat rats, not dogs.

—I have ordered where the dog must be! —Grandma shouted.

—Calm down, Mom. I'm going to take him back to the basement —my mother said, attracted by the screams.

Grandma left. Her bad action of the day was done, and she could feel happy about that.

—Can I go with you this time, Mom? —I asked.

—No, I'll go alone. Don't worry, Jo, nothing will happen to him in the basement. He was there once; he can go back again —my mother consoled me.

But just before they separated Ps from my side, something happened that saved my little dog, and made everyone forget about the rats... at least for a while: The doorbell rang. We looked out the window and saw something totally new to us.

On the porch of the house stood a plump girl, with tiny braids glued to her face. She was a redhead, full of freckles, and frankly, ugly. But above all, she was careless. She was exactly the kind of girl that Grandma would dislike just by looking at her. Right away I had a good hunch about her.

Anyways, you could barely see the girl. In front of, around and behind her there were many trunks of different sizes and colors.

I would have given anything to see the face of Grandma when she opened the door. It's a shame I was upstairs in my room, and that I didn't see it. I saw, however –because I ran down the stairs–, her surprise when the chubby girl entered the house.

She came in as if it were her home. She didn't say «hello» or «please» or any other nonsense that Grandma likes so much. She only entered, pulling a trunk that, from what I could tell, was full of little trunks inside. Behind the girl came a man who almost ran over me.

–Where is your Mom? –he asked.

The bill collectors always do that. As soon as they see me, they ask about my parents.

I pointed to Grandma. The man greeted her and left her a piece of paper.

–This is the taxi charge, ma'am. Sign here.

Grandma signed, but automatically. She took a breath and, when the man left, tried to recover from her amazement.

–You must be Alina, right? –she said, and approached her, but with such a clumsy step that she ended up stumbling over a trunk and fell.

Alina didn't flinch. Grandma, from the floor, seemed to boil with fury, but held back as best as she could.

–What are all these trunks? –she asked.

For every answer, Alina howled. An ugly and long howl, like a dog that turns into a wolf under a full moon.

Boni ran down the stairs.

–Is this your trunk collection? –she turned to Alina.

Alina didn't respond.

–What are you talking about, Boni? –Mom asked.

–José, Alina's grandfather, just called. He explained that Alina would arrive with her collection of trunks. He mentioned that he hoped it wasn't a problem.

–Of course it's not –Grandma composed herself–. It's just…
we would have wanted to know in advance; we would have
gone to the airport to pick you up.

–I took a taxi –Alina growled.

–Yes, I know that –Grandma looked at the taxi driver's
receipt, which still remained in her hand, and she sighed–.
Well, we have a custard for welcoming you –Grandma pointed
to the kitchen–. Are you hungry?

As an answer, Alina went to the kitchen. When I approached
her, she had already put her hands into the custard and was
eating it like that, without a spoon or plate. Grandma almost
had a heart attack, but I was delighted.

–Please, Alina, wash your hands. Would you? –asked
Grandma.

Alina looked at her hands, as if to check how dirty they were.
She determined that they weren't so bad, and continued eating.

Grandma took the opportunity to introduce the whole family.

–In this house we are five…

–Six –I corrected.

–For now, five –Grandma said, widening her eyes.

But you could see Alina didn't care at all how many we were.
She barely heard our names when Grandma introduced us. She
finished the custard in a heartbeat. Not showing any kind of
concern, and without asking if she was even allowed to, she
opened the refrigerator and grabbed the apple pie, which was
our dessert for the night. She broke it in half, sniffed it a little,
and stuffed one of the two pieces into her mouth in one bite.
The rest, she put in one of her overall pockets. She left the room
and, while still chewing, began carrying her trunks upstairs.

Grandma was very upset, but her manners didn't allow her
to say anything. Alina was a guest and not a part of her house,

so she had no way to blackmail her. Mom was stunned by the situation. On the other hand, I was full of the joys of spring.

–How long is… –Grandma looked for the words, and in the end decided on her name– Alina staying with us?

–She is here for a month.

–One month! –sighed Grandma.

An immense rumble in the living room occurred: Alina had tried to take her trunks upstairs, but the stairs were too steep and she fell back down.

Grandma hesitated to help her. My mother didn't. She approached Alina and offered her a hand to get up. Alina howled as an answer.

–Aren't you going to pick her up, Magdalena?

–She doesn't want me to. And if she doesn't want…

It was obvious that my mother didn't know how to treat Alina. No one knew.

That's when Granny Trina showed up. She looked at Alina lying on the floor with her feet in the air, surrounded by half-open trunks, but she wasn't surprised or anything. She assumed it was the most normal thing in the world. Sometimes, I wonder what world Granny Trina lives in.

–Oh! But it's eucalyptus wood!

–What? –Grandma stammered.

–What? –repeated my mother.

–That trunk. It's made of eucalyptus wood –reaffirmed Granny.

Alina, in response, extended her hand to our great-grandmother.

–Come with me, my dear, I'll show you to your room. Have you tried the Catalan cream that I made? –Granny Trina asked.

–It was delicious –Alina declared.

We were all shocked with surprise.

Grandma turned red with rage –from not having something under her control– and you could almost see how her stomach was boiling with anger.

–Who does she think she is! –muttered Grandma between her teeth.

Boni was very upset. Her point was that if she, who lived here, couldn't talk like that to Grandma, why could Alina. But I loved it. I saw Grandma swallow her tongue for the first time and that put me in a very good mood. I hadn't felt so well since when Dad lived with us.

IX.

With all the hubbub and preparations for Alina's arrival, I hadn't found the time to open my father's letter. I wanted to open his letter once it was extremely calm around me, for being able to dive deep into the meaning of each word.

The day after Alina's arrival, I woke up so early that I had to go downstairs and turn on the light in the living room to read his letter, because it hadn't yet dawned. Everyone else was sleeping; there was an uncommon tranquility in the house, and I assumed it was the best time to open the letter.

In the brief lines he had written to me, Dad said how much he missed me and that he didn't know when he could return, but that he was saving all the money he earned to buy a house for the four of us, where both Boni and I were each going to have a room of our own.

Suddenly I felt sadness. A much deeper one than when Dad had left: I wasn't sure I remembered his face.

It was all Grandma's fault. She was the one who had thrown Dad out of the house, the one who had made our lives miserable.

I started thinking, I don't know why, how different my life would be, if instead of being the granddaughter of my grandmother and being imprisoned in this family, I was a little street orphan who sang on the sidewalks to be able to survive.

I would only have one outfit. I'm sure that I would become friends with some old beggar who had a can so that people could throw in money whenever I sang. We would spend all day working; he, with the can extended towards the people; and I, singing sad songs. And people would walk by and look at my old and disheveled clothes and would say: «poor little girl, she has no parents, she has no grandmothers». But I wouldn't feel sad, but happy, because I would be free.

Little by little, while I was thinking about this, I took off the clothes that I had on. I took out of the laundry basket the dirty clothes which Boni had worn to clean the house. They were full of dust and cobwebs, and very frayed. I put them on. Without making any noise, I opened the front door. The wood creaked a little. Alina, who was lying on the couch, raised her head.

–Where are you going?

It was the first time she spoke to me.

–Why aren't you sleeping? –I questioned her.

–It's day time in Russia right now… I'm not sleepy. Where are you going? –she was insistent.

I remembered how she ate the desserts from Granny Trina all by herself.

–It's not your problem.

–Can I go with you?

–No –I said, and closed the door.

In front of our house there is a café. Sometimes, if it's really early, and there still aren't any other smells, you can catch a whiff of freshly baked bread. This morning was like that, warm and odorous. I remembered that I hadn't eaten breakfast. But I didn't feel like I wanted to return. I didn't want to face Grandma, in case she was already awake. Actually, I didn't want to see her ever again. Therefore, while I decided what to do with my life, I sat on the edge of the sidewalk, next to the café.

I sat there, disheveled, with dirty clothes, feeling quite unhappy, when some kids approached me. They were four; three were still toddlers, but the biggest, who I could tell was the leader, was as tall as a stick and had a boomerang in his hand.

I had never touched a boomerang. I had seen them in photos, I had even read about them, that when you throw them, they always return to where you are, and that they were invented by people in Australia. But to touch one, and to throw it myself so that it would come back to me, that I had never done.

I paid all my attention to the boomerang. The boy who was throwing it didn't let the other toddlers touch it. He threw it with a certain movement of his elbow; he tried hard, but the boomerang never returned to him.

The youngest ones began to mock him.

–You don't know how to do it, Reni –remarked one.

–Give it to me, I know how to do it –another demanded.

–Shut up, you don't know anything –threatened Reni–. Leave it to me or I'll slap you!

The toddlers left him alone. But when they saw Reni was still unable to get the boomerang to return to him, they continued their taunting.

Meanwhile, I was drawing in the dust on the sidewalk. I drew something I had seen in one of the books about indigenous people that my Spanish professor had. That book had paintings that were created by the aborigines of Australia. I always liked it because they drew like I do, which means, they didn't know how to draw pretty things. And even so, those paintings were famous.

—Eh, you, what are you doing?

The one that they called Reni was talking to me.

—I am drawing.

—What are you drawing?

—Drawings of the aborigines from Australia. They believed there is magic in these images —I explained, proud of my knowledge on the subject.

—Reni, she's doing magic —said one brat.

—Stop drawing —suddenly ordered the one they called Reni.

—Why?

—Because I say so.

What? I had run away from home so I could feel free and already in my first hour of freedom a brat was giving me commands!

—I do what I want, not what you tell me to do.

—Is that right? Now you'll see! Either you stop drawing, or I'll throw this at you.

—You don't know how to throw that anyway —I said, and stood up.

I was bigger than the other three brats, but not more than Reni. He was much taller than me, though thinner.

The brats made fun of him because of my bold answer. Reni, then, took the boomerang, and I'm sure he thought about hitting me with it, but I tackled him first:

—*Guanacabibes*! —I screamed with all my strength and jumped on top of Reni.

We both fell down. I caught the boomerang and hit him with all my strength. The three brats jumped on me, attacking me at the same time. Although they were smaller than me, they were three, and they hit me really hard. I didn't stop kicking and punching, mostly the air. I bit one of them on the leg, but the other two hit me until I released the boomerang. As soon as Reni was able to, he took the boomerang. When he was about to hit me with it, Alina appeared out of nowhere! And she jumped on him.

Alina, who is so much plumper than me, knocked the breath out of him. She took the boomerang from Reni and stood next to me. You could see that she was willing to hit whoever approached us. The brats were already tired after the few punches that I was able to give them, and now we were two against them.

Alina, so plump and fearless, scared them.

You could see they wanted to attack us, but they were hesitating.

–Give us the boomerang and we'll go –Reni said, finally.

–Get out of here, or I'll stick your boomerang in your head –said Alina, while showing him her fist.

The day was beginning to dawn. Some cars were passing by; there were people already entering into the café. Reni looked at the brats.

–Let's move on.

Without taking his eyes off of us, he began to move away.

Before he disappeared completely, Alina threw him the boomerang. It fell at his feet. He picked it up, threatened us with it, but didn't approach. Then, we saw him get lost amongst the people who were beginning to populate the block. The three other brats were with him.

Alina looked at me. I was bleeding from my nose. And I was crying, I think more out of anger than from anything else. I didn't like that she saw me like that, but she didn't make fun of me or anything. Instead, she requested:

–Come with me, now!

She grabbed my hand, started running and pulled me along with her. I wanted to ask her why we were running, but I couldn't; to cry kept me from speaking.

—We have to keep moving —I heard her say—. When one is sad and stays still, sadness is worse. You have to move, move!

We arrived at the coast. The sea was calm and clear. As the sun hadn't come out completely, the palm trees left long shadows on the beach.

I wasn't crying anymore.

—Come on, let's go to the water, you have to wash the blood from your nose —said Alina.

I let myself go in her command. We walked into the water up to our knees. She crouched down and cupped her hands. She told me to put my face in her hands. I bent down. A little red trickle was coming out of my nose and it mixed in her hands with the water of the sea.

—Now, throw your head back and hold your nose —she ordered me—. It works! —she announced, a little surprised.

When the blood stopped coming out, I asked her:

—Shouldn't you wash yourself, too?

—I'm not dirty.

—You're covered in dust. Let me, I'll wash you.

I pushed her red hair back and wiped her face with my wet hands. She had so many freckles, that you couldn't tell the difference between them and the dirt. I bathed her as much as possible, but she had a thick crust behind her ears.

—Do you ever shower? —I asked.

—Saturdays —she answered, as if it were the most natural thing in the world.

On the way back home, we held hands.

Once at home, she showed me her collection of trunks. They were made of all kinds of wood, and she talked about them until, little by little, the people of the house started to wake up, and it was time for breakfast.

X.

–What are we going to do today? –Alina asked me.

At that time, she was only speaking to me and Granny Trina. In spite of how much Boni tried to talk to her, my sister only received long silences as a response. Boni tried to hide it, but the truth is, it bothered her. As the most intelligent student in her class that she was, Boni wasn't accustomed to being ignored.

Precisely because of this situation, I felt responsible to take care of Alina. Also, it's not that it was a problem. Beyond her opposition to cleanliness, she wasn't a bad person.

–There is something I want to do… –I announced, mysteriously, to Alina–. If you want, you can come with me.

–What is it? –she inquired.

–Can I go with you? –implored Boni.

I had the desire to say no to my sister, that she couldn't come with us. She had given me the toddler treatment so many times that she totally deserved it. But I felt sorry for her, so intelligent and always disciplined, and now being openly rejected by our cousin.

–Well, you can come. But I need you to not have any problem with getting dirty.

–No problem here.

–And you can't bring a book with you.

Boni always carried a book wherever she went.

It was her way of avoiding boredom, in case she didn't find anything interesting to do.

–But…

–You won't get bored.

–What are we waiting for? –prompted Alina.

I jumped out of bed and started packing for the adventure. I took a few tools and some of Dad's clothes.

–What are you doing with Dad's clothes? –protested Boni.

–Dad has a lot of them, he won't mind if we take some. Now: let's go!

I took Boni and Alina to the beach. Once we got there, I started to look along the horizon.

–What are you looking for?

–I'm looking for an abandoned wood house.

Alina got excited.

–Is there one out here?

–No, Alina, it's just one of Jo's inventions.

But Boni had to eat her words.

–There it is! –I announced, pointing to it.

–That thing?

I started to run toward the wood house. Alina and Boni, behind me. True: it didn't look like a house anymore. If I hadn't known the story of the sullen old man that Mr. Hamze told me about, I wouldn't have identified those wooden ruins. Where once there was a house, there now was just a wooden wall, almost destroyed. And there wasn't the slightest trace of a garden with poppies and sunflowers.

–What's this? –asked Boni, as she approached with difficulty: she wasn't accustomed to running in sand.

I narrated Boni the story that Mr. Hamze had told me. Like me, when Mr. Hamze finished telling his memories of the old man, Boni remained in silence for a while.

–What do you want to do with what's left of this house? –she wanted to know, when she finally spoke.

–With the house, nothing. What I want to do is to plant a scarecrow over here... one similar to the one that the old man once built.

The face of Boni reflected surprise. Contrary to what I expected from her, she thought it was a very good idea. Mr. Hamze's story had transformed her into another person: She told me she would help me build the scarecrow.

However, I had no idea how to build a scarecrow. Boni could see that, but, unlike so many other times, she didn't scoff. You could really notice a change in her.

–We need a body for the scarecrow –she commented, and I noticed the use of the plural form.

I lifted a log from the ground.

–Do you think this could work as the main structure for the body?

Alina and Boni knelt down and began to dig a hole in the sand, so the log would stay firmly in the ground. I was about put it in the hole, when Boni stopped me.

–Wait, Jo; first you have to nail on a cross board, so the scarecrow has arms.

How strange and yet how nice it was to have Boni on my side. If I had only known that one story was needed…

We ended up dirty, sweaty, and tanned by the sun of the beach.

I had crushed my index finger with a hammer blow, and it hurt a lot. But the scarecrow was standing, and he looked very firm in the sand. He was wearing Dad's clothes; he seemed real, especially from a distance.

–Should we say something? –Boni had the idea.

–Something like what?

–I don't know, but I feel we must tell him something… –she cleared her throat and pronounced, solemnly–: Lord Scarecrow, we have built you in the name of Mr. Hamze, and in memory of the elder who lived in the house that existed here.

–Is that it? –I asked, after a few minutes of silence.

–Yes –she said, simply.

—I'm hungry —announced Alina—. Can we return to the house? Granny Trina should have new desserts…

When Grandma saw us come back, we looked like three little balls of dirt. Especially Alina. If Grandma wouldn't have been so entertained with talking to the mailman, tremendous reprimand would have been ours! But because she was very focused on the mailman, Alina went directly to the kitchen and Boni and I skirted the garden, without sorrows or glories.

—Come, I want you to see something —I said to Boni.

—What is it?

As an answer, I pointed to a mound of earth. She looked as if she didn't understand.

—Mr. Hamze gave me a seed, and I planted it there. I don't know if it was a poppy seed, or sunflower seed, like that one the old man had planted in front of his house…

—Are you talking about the seed that they gave you along with Ps?

—Yes.

—It's an avocado.

—How do you know?

—I know how to recognize an avocado seed when I see it.

Alina greeted us from inside the house. She had a big pot in her hands, for sure a custard from Granny Trina.

Boni immediately went inside of the house. I stayed outside for a while looking at the mound of earth. Beyond what plant it would be, under that mound of earth there was life growing, and I liked that.

XI.

When the mailman left, Grandma gave us the reprimand of the century. I didn't pay much attention, because I was tired from working on the beach, but I did hear something about being punished for a thousand years, with its thousand days and thousand nights.

Later, while I was napping, I heard Grandma complain about the rats in the basement.

I dreamed about them. They were preparing a party and I had been invited. I just didn't have anyone to go with me. Alina went with Boni; Norah with her father, and I wanted to go with mine, but I couldn't find him. I wanted to write him a letter for him to return from Russia, so he could go with me to the party, but the paper got tangled up in my hands and I couldn't untangle it, no matter how hard I tried.

When I woke up it was nighttime. Boni and Alina were getting dressed.

–What are you doing?

–Hello, sleepy girl.

–We're going to a party.

–What? And when did you think of waking me up to tell me?

–There was no need to wake you up. You woke yourself up –my sister snapped.

Apparently, Boni had gone back to the same old attitude. And now she was getting along just fine with Alina.

–What party is that? –I asked as I got up and opened the closet to get dressed.

–Norah's party. She came to invite us a while ago.

In the closet I couldn't find any clothes that I liked.

–Aren't we still grounded? –I was still waking up and I was a little confused about what was a dream and what was real.

–Since when do you do what Grandma tells you to?

–I was just checking.

I put on shorts, boots and a pullover.

–Are you going to a party in boots?

–Do you want to see the other pair of shoes that I have?

–No, thanks.

–They were the ones I took to the beach today.

–I already imagined that.

–With the boots it will be easier to climb out the window –commented Alina.

And it was true. Because they were so tough, I could rely on the nooks of the balcony without hurting my feet.

But they definitely weren't very functional at the party. The uptight friend of Norah and Mr. Hamze didn't stop looking at me and laughing. All for those damn boots. I didn't imagine the riffraff that would be at the party. Those who weren't from England, were pretending to be from there. They wore scarves, although it was as hot as a thousand demons. They spoke with a British accent; some of them pretended better than others. If I hadn't felt so out of place, I would have thought it was fun to see them all trying to be and behave in a way they really weren't.

Norah, who normally was a fine girl, was smoking, like Mr. Hamze. The smoke that came direct from her mouth floated in the room, above the music. She was also trying to be someone she wasn't. That bothered me to the core.

I would have turned around, put on my boots and gone in the direction of my house, if it hadn't been for that smell.

It was my favorite smell in the world. It came to me suddenly, and it took me away from people who pretended to be more glamorous, who laughed without end, without having anything funny in front of them. It took me away from feeling hot just by seeing so many scarves and coats, as if the weather wasn't the usual 35 degrees Celsius. I didn't know where the smell was coming from, and at first, I didn't even know what it was.

I got up and started to follow it. Like the smoke from Norah's cigar, the essence of the smell floated above music and people. It took me to the kitchen, but it didn't stay there. It was flowing from outside of the house. I went out.

In the doorway, there was Norah and some of her uptight friends. They were asking Alina, with irony and bad vibes, about her collection of trunks. Alina began to explain, but when she realized that they considered her crazy, she began to growl.

I looked fiercely at Norah. She noticed, and approached me, with an innocent attitude.

–What? We are just playing.

I didn't say anything. I was disappointed inside, yes. But I didn't think too much about it; the smell was again floating next to me, now with more strength. I followed it.

Norah got between the smell and me.

–Jo, sorry. You're right, I've behaved like an idiot. Sometimes I just want to fit in, you understand?

–Yes –I said. But what you call understanding, to truly understand another's behavior, no, I didn't understand her.

However, she was glad.

–I'm going inside to take off my scarf –she informed me–. I'm dying of heat.

Norah entered her house. The party was its peak. I saw Boni dancing; she wasn't bad at it.

I sat on the sidewalk in front of Norah's house. After a while, Alina sat down next to me.

The smell was gone now. I had no choice but to sit down and wait for it to return. Meanwhile, I spoke.

–You know, Alina, Grandma is going to know that we came to a party. It's too noisy for her not to realize it, and as it's in Norah's house, she's going to imagine that she invited us. In this moment she must be waiting for us to return...

–That doesn't bother me.

–You will also be punished.

Then I saw who Alina really was: she told me her thoughts.

She thought that, for as bad as life with Grandma was, it was much better than living in a family where there is nothing but silence and sadness. And that was what she had in Russia. Her grandfather José barely spoke to her, he almost didn't pay attention to anyone. Her mother, José's daughter, had remarried and lived with her new husband and new children in another city, far away from Moscow. She lived alone with her grandfather, but since he barely speaks, and is frequently absorbed in his own mind, she felt lonely all the time.

–At least –Alina said– your grandmother cares about you. She yells at you and scolds you, but because she cares.

Because Alina's grandfather didn't know if she bathed, or cried, or went to school or didn't; if she stole food in a store, didn't sleep at home, or had a collection of trunks or scarecrows. To her grandfather nothing matters, because the war had taken away from him the joy of life. Forever.

–Maybe –I looked at Alina– you can stay and live with us.

–I cannot –she said, and I saw then the exact person she was–. I can't leave Grandpa alone for too long.

XII.

That night, I didn't experience again the same smell that had previously captivated me. I waited for it in vain; never arrived.

When Boni got tired of wiggling her body, she found Alina and me; by then we were lying on the sidewalk at the corner of Norah's house. Boni arrived with a serious face; she asked us if we were ready to leave. She looked tired.

–Did you have a good time?

–The party wasn't too bad. But now comes the worst part.

I knew what she meant. If Grandma had already punished us for a thousand years with its thousand days and nights, what punishment could be worse now?

But I'd had time to think of a plan:

–If you want to have a quiet night, do exactly what I'm going to tell you.

Boni and Alina looked at me, impressed. I got up from the sidewalk and walked towards the house. Boni and Alina followed me. Then, I explained my plan:

–We can't enter the house using the path we took for getting out. And we can't enter through the main door: the timbers in the room creak... so, Grandma could wake up...

Sometimes Boni was so innocent...

–Grandma is already awake. I bet you the scarecrow that she is waiting for us in the bedroom.

–What should we do, then? –Alina said. Only a few days with us and she was already afraid of our grandmother. I have to admit it: Grandma was very effective in her monarchy.

–Follow me –I told them.

They followed, obediently, behind me. We entered into the living room. Near the door were Alina's trunks, which were so large, that it hadn't been possible to take them upstairs. I opened the first one.

–Boni, enter here.

–Is this your plan?

–Nobody is going to look for us in a trunk. We are inside the house, but we are not visible.

Boni entered without arguing.

–It may work…

When I was opening the second trunk, so that Alina and I could sleep in there, a little light came on in the living room. It was Grandma.

–Good evening to the fugitives.

We were all stunned. I would have run, but the surprise didn't leave me.

–I was waiting for all of you in the bedroom when, suddenly, I remembered how imaginative you are, Jo.

It was a compliment, but it sounded like a razor shaving my neck.

Grandma got up from the couch. I could see, hanging as long it was, the belt which she had in her hand. I had seen that before, and I didn't like it.

Suddenly, without knowing what I was doing, (later I understood it as a preservation instinct) I jumped over the trunks, in the direction of the door. Boni and Alina looked at me; I'm almost sure they wanted to go with me, but they were too scared. I was too, but my legs moved on their own, like springs independent from my mind.

And my legs took me, running, outside. With immense strides I flew through the garden, jumped the fence of the house, crossed the street, passed the café, and even the street after that. I looked back briefly, before losing the house to the horizon. Grandma was standing at the door, but she was already very far away and I didn't know what the expression on her face was. In any case, I could guess.

I kept running.

I'm not sure how I ended up at the old, wood house, where the scarecrow was. I was hungry, and I was tired, but what tormented me most was that without me in the house, I didn't know who would take care of Ps. Because I didn't intend to ever return to that home. At least not while Dad wasn't there.

I lay down at the feet of the scarecrow, as if I myself was a delivery for the sullen old man from the story of Mr. Hamze. The sound of the sea on the beach, a few meters from the scarecrow, obscured all the other noises of the night.

I fell asleep.

XIII.

When I woke up, I didn't immediately open my eyes. I used all the other senses to understand what was happening around me. One thing was for sure: I was in someone's arms. A person was carrying me, and that person was walking at a hurried pace.

The memories of the previous day rushed into my mind. I thought that maybe, in the middle of the cold of the night, and because of hunger, I had died and now death was coming to take me. I thought about how much my father would miss me when he realized he had lost his daughter. Even Mom and Boni would mourn my death. Some tears must have come out with these thoughts.

—She's already awake —said Boni, or maybe it was Death, with a similar voice.

I opened my eyes. It was Mom who was carrying me. Boni and Alina were behind her.

—Where are we going?

—We are going to take you to our house, my girl.

—I don't want to go to that house anymore, Mom.

—Don't worry about your grandmother. Everything will be different now.

We got home. No trace of Grandma anywhere. It wasn't that I wanted to see her, either. Mom climbed the stairs with me in her arms, and left me in my bed, gently.

—I'm going to bring you something to eat, Jo. You must be hungry.

The bed was so comfortable. There's nothing like sleeping on the ground to appreciate one's bed. Boni and Alina were attending to me.

–What happened when I left? –I interrogated them.

–Everybody woke up. We looked for you everywhere –Alina told me.

–Did you worry about me? –I asked Boni.

–I knew I was going to find you –she said–. And I was right.

–You almost didn't find me. I was about to leave forever.

–You wanted to be found. You put yourself in a place where you knew we could find you –she said, and began to read–. I was certain we would find you, so I didn't worry.

She opened her book, and immediately appeared to be absorbed in her reading.

Alina came up to me.

–She was worried –she revealed, very softly–. She looked for you everywhere… she was the one who had the idea of going where we built the scarecrow.

I looked at Boni. She hid her feelings with a yawn.

I wanted to know where Grandma was, but I didn't feel like asking about her. Instead, I remembered Ps.

–Where is Ps?

Boni and Alina looked at me, startled. They hadn't thought about Ps. All of a sudden, I was on my feet.

–I have to look for him! I don't know how long he's been without food!

Boni left the book under her pillow:

–Alina, you look for him downstairs, I'll take care of this floor. Jo, you should remain resting in here. Besides, Mom is going to bring you breakfast very soon…

They left the room. Despite what Boni had told me, I got up and looked outside. The garden! Boni hadn't said anything about looking in the garden! I immediately climbed out the window.

XIV

I let myself drop into the garden. I could see from there that Alina was examining under every piece of furniture in the living room, and how Boni was looking inside the oven, in the kitchen. Mom and Granny Trina were also looking everywhere; they seemed to be alarmed.

Grandma, on the other hand, wasn't anywhere to be seen. Maybe she had decided to leave after all, from that house where she felt uncomfortable, amongst people who shouted as much as the rats that, according to her, were living in the basement.

«Rats!», I thought, and a chill ran down my back. Maybe Grandma had taken Ps into the basement! I imagined my little Ps, being devoured by hundreds of hungry rats.

I didn't think about taking a weapon to fight with the rats or to ask anyone for help; not even the possibility that a rat would bite me: I ran into the basement.

Even if I had been thinking for a thousand years, I would never have imagined what I was about to find there. The first thing that caught my attention in the basement was that the lights were on.

Grandma, so strict with order, never left a light on in a room where there wasn't any person. Unless Grandma was already there in the basement. But it was unlikely, because that was a place for junk and humidity, and she wouldn't stay in such a reprehensible place.

I entered, stealthily. There were a lot of books open everywhere. I picked one up. It said:

Российская Федерация

Slowly, I read: Rossíiskaya Federátsiya. I didn't know what it meant (I only know how to read Russian; I don't understand what the words mean). But I did know something: the rats weren't the ones that were living in the basement.

In that moment, to confirm my hunch, the scent arrived. It was the same one I had smelled the night before, at Norah's house (already it seemed to be a night very distant in time).

—Dad? —I heard myself asking.

Silence. The perfume became stronger; a dark silhouette appeared in a corner of the basement.

—Daddy… —I approached him, wistfully.

—Jo —he stepped into the light–. Jo!

I jumped on top of him. His beard was rough, and it pricked me.

—Josefina, you found me! —he said.

From my Dad's mouth, my name doesn't sound so bad.

—Your perfume. I could recognize that smell among all the smells of the world.

I abandoned myself in his arms. I was there, without moving, submerged in his embrace, until I thought I heard the whimpering of a dog. Then I remembered.

—Dad, have you seen my puppy?

—It's around here; I built a little house for him and he seems to like it.

Daddy took a couple steps, moved a box, and pulled out Ps. He was wrapped in a blanket and was chewing on a bone.

—I named him Ps, Dad.

—I know that. Your mother has kept me informed of everything. I've given him some food, because I know you've been busy…

—Have you spent a lot of time down here?

—Some weeks.

—Why didn't you tell me, Dad?

At that moment, we felt that someone was approaching.

–Dad –I whispered–. Should we hide?

I had realized that my father had been living in the basement all this time, precisely to hide himself from Grandma.

But Dad didn't have time to respond. Someone had already entered the basement and confidently walked between the boxes of books, wood and other junk, towards us. It was Mom. When she saw that Dad was holding me in his arms, she sighed with relief.

–There you are, Jo! I thought you may have escaped again.

–It's okay. She's with me –Dad hugged me.

–You're not going to hide anymore, are you Dad?

–No –my mother was the one that replied–. Like I told you, Jo, things are going to be different from now on.

Boni arrived, running, behind my mother.

–Does Jo already know?

Suddenly, I realized that Boni knew that our father was living in the basement. I wanted to scream with rage, but something stopped the words, which disappeared before leaving my throat.

Grandma was standing at the basement door. The sun of summer, intense, reflected her shadow down the stairs, that stretched almost to where we were.

Boni became nervous:

–It's my fault; she must have followed me.

I sank deeper into Dad's embrace. However, Dad assumed it as something natural and even expected. He let me down gently and left the basement where he had hidden for weeks, as naturally as if he came out of a shower. Mom, Boni and I went after him.

Alina and Granny Trina later commented on how stupefied they were when they saw us coming out of the basement, sprouting as if we were plants. And it really was a weird picture to see us all in the garden; Alina and Granny Trina a little apart; Dad, Mom, Boni and I, a compact mass, facing Grandma.

The only one who wasn't tense was Dad. He didn't pay too much attention to Grandma. Showing a very relaxed smile, he gave me a little nudge on my shoulder.

–What about if all of you go to your room and grab what you need for spending the day at the beach? Does that idea interest you?

It seemed fantastic to me, but I looked at my grandmother. She was stiff like a stake. It was clear that she wasn't happy to see my Dad, but she didn't say a word. I bet that at that point she was processing the idea of how the noises from the basement weren't rats at all, but my father.

–That's a fantastic idea, Daniel –said Mom–. Jo, you heard your father, go to the room. You too, Boni. Alina, are you coming with us?

–No –Alina answered with her mouth full. Even in a tense and atypical moment like this one she had a dessert from Granny Trina in her mouth–. I'm eating.

Despite my mother's order, I didn't move. My father approached me:

–From now on things are going to be different, Jo –he spoke, looking at me, but I had the feeling that he wasn't talking to me–. Enough of living with fear. That isn't right. Your grandmother knows that if things don't change, she will be left alone.

–I wouldn't be alone; Trina is with me –Grandma replied imperceptibly.

–You never know what you've got till it's gone –murmured Granny Trina, moving her head.

I went to the room and chose the cutest of all my swimsuits: a flowered bikini that Dad had given me last year. I grabbed for Ps (I wasn't leaving him) a pullover that was small enough to fit him just right.

We went with Ps to the beach. The sun was very strong, and there were many people under the shade of palm trees. But we weren't afraid of the sun. We wanted to take advantage of every drop of water. Mom was all made up; she looked radiant even when the sea began to leave black stripes under her eyes. Boni took care of Ps the whole time. She left me alone with Dad, and I must say that I really enjoyed it.

I showed Dad where I had passed the night when I left home. He thought it was great that I had slept under the scarecrow. He didn't bother, not even a little bit, that I had taken his clothes to dress the scarecrow.

–So, tell me, Jo –asked Dad–, what would you like to do now? Would you like to go to the café by the house, to eat one of those sweet-smelling pastries?

I hadn't had any breakfast, so I was quite hungry.

–Can we? –I was full of joy.

–Sure! Let's go!

–Mmmm… You know what, Dad? Later. Not now. Let's stay here a little longer. It's very pleasant.

–All right, then. As you want.

–Hee-hee –I laughed.

XV.

When we came back from the beach, I did eat, in the café and in the house, mountains of pastries. Afterwards, I slept for what felt like two years, the quietest dream I'd had since Dad had gone to Russia. I kept thinking that they perfectly could have informed me when he returned; I wouldn't have said anything to Grandma about him living in the basement, but I understood that they considered me a little girl, and the best thing to prevent this was to not make a fuss about it. So, I stayed calm, without to fight anyone. Also, I didn't feel like fighting. I was the happiest girl for having my father at home.

When I awoke from the long sleep, it was getting dark. The sun's light was still hot enough, but everything had a beautiful orange calm.

I left through the window for the garden (for by then I had learned how to do it very well). Dad and Mom were in the living room. They were organizing Alina's trunks. They looked happy.

In the garden, I went to the place where I had done my Black Magic in the Arawak language. The magic had worked. Grandma was neutralized. Everything was better than ever.

I noticed that where I had planted the avocado seed there was a tiny plant, fragile, recently born from the Earth. It was there, light green, as small as a fingernail of mine. It looked beautiful. I spent a long time watching it. I thought of the sullen, old man who knew Mr. Hamze: Sometimes, when you are looking at something you love, you feel like you want to sing.

So, I sang to the plant. First some stanzas of popular songs, then I started to invent new tunes, in what I thought was the Arawak language (which I use for more than magic).

When my mother came to the garden, she found me lying down, singing to the flimsy plant that was recently born.

–Jo, what are you doing with that tiny plant?

–I'm singing to it in the Arawak language.

–Oh, my girl.

My mother, as usual, so dramatic. She knows how to turn everything into a soap opera.

–Jo, let's go out. Go to the bathroom and wash your hands, we are going out.

–But, Mom. Can't you see I'm busy?

–Jo, to the bathroom. Now!

Mom looked like she was about to boil over. I went without delay to the bathroom. I did all I could to clean the dirt from my hands, but I wasn't successful; when I came back to Mom, I still had dirt under my fingernails.

–Come here, Jo –my mother called as she added saliva to a handkerchief. She cleaned under my fingernails.

–Do you know where we're going, Jo?

–No…

–I'm going to take you to the psychologist.

What? Where was that coming from?

–Do you know why I'm going to take you to the psychologist, Jo?

I couldn't think of any reason.

–Because of what you wrote in your assignment for your Spanish professor.

Because of the paragraph I wrote for Brick Head? Was that the only reason?

–I had already forgotten about that –I said, and I was being honest.

–Well, I remember it, Jo! Also… we need to go because of everything that you've been writing in your journal all this time.

–Have you read my journal?
But Mom didn't respond.

XVI.

The psychologist turned out to be an older man. He smiled at me as soon as we came inside the room.

–How can I help you today?

–You'll see, doctor. My daughter has problems –she pointed at me.

–You think so? She seems pretty fine to me.

I liked that psychologist right away.

–Look –my mother began–. She opened her purse and took out… my journal!

What was my mother doing with my journal? Obviously, she had read it.

–This notebook is Jo's diary. She writes…

–Yes?

My mother couldn't find the words. The doctor encouraged her.

–It's common to have a diary at that age…

–Look, doctor, in this notebook Jo, my daughter…

–Yes?

–Here in this journal she has written about Alina, a cousin of hers. She wrote that Alina came to visit her and that they went to a party together.

–That's common at those ages, ma'am.

–It's… maybe I can't explain myself.

And she was right. She wasn't explaining herself at all. I was the only one who knew what she wanted to say, but I didn't intend to help her say it.

–You'll see, doctor… Alina… she doesn't exist. My daughter doesn't have any relative with that name.

–How come...?

–She... invented her. She invented Alina, she even invented a puppy that it says in here she received from a neighbor of ours, a neighbor called Mr. Hamze. But, you'll see, doctor... we don't have any neighbor with that name!

The doctor leaned forward and looked at me with all his attention.

You could see that he found me very interesting.

–Ma'am, would you wait outside for a moment?

–Is it necessary? –asked my mother.

–Yes. Please –the psychologist insisted, and indicated the door to her, with a polite but determined gesture.

–Should I leave this with you? –my mother was pointing at my journal.

–Not with me. That notebook is not mine. It belongs to your daughter. I think you should leave it with her.

–Sure...

My mother gave me my journal and left the room.

The psychologist waited for my mother to close the door. He stood up, opened a small refrigerator that was on a mahogany table, and pulled out a juice.

–Would you like one?

–Yes.

We drank a couple of sips in unison.

–Well, tell me, what's Alina like? –he snapped all of a sudden.

–My grandmother doesn't like her –I said, and I don't know why but, I smiled.

–Is it hard to find someone your grandmother likes? –he asked me, in an accomplice tone.

–Almost impossible –I declared.

–Your grandmother will be quite alone.

–Well, no... Because she has a big house. And my parents don't.

–Is this grandmother the mother of your mother?

–Yes.

–And how does your dad get along with your grandmother?

–My dad is on a work trip right now.

–Where?

–Russia.

–And when he is at home, how does he deal with her?

–He's saving to buy a house for just us. Us means for Boni, my mom and me.

–Mmm.

–What do you mean with «Mmm»?

The psychologist smiled.

–I also had a similar grandmother –he confessed.

–You don't know my grandmother. Mine is worse than yours.

–It's possible.

I liked that psychologist.

–Did you have a good time while you were writing?

–A great time! In my family almost nothing ever happens, but in my journal, a lot of things happen every day!

–I wouldn't call it a journal.

What did he mean?

–I would call it a novel, more specifically, an autobiographical novel, because even if it's fiction, it's based on your life.

–The writers are the ones who write novels.

–I suppose that makes you a writer, then.

Then I was the one that smiled. I think it was my first smile since my dad had left.

–Hee-hee –I chuckled.

–Hee-hee? –he was surprised.

–It's something between my dad and me –I explained–. When he says something and I laugh like that: «Hee-hee», he knows that I liked what he said, and that I'm very happy.

–Oh, I understand!

And you could see that he understood! He was a very good psychologist.

–Would you call your mom now, Jo? She must be desperate out there –he said and winked at me.

And he was right: my mother looked very impatient and worried.

–How is my little girl? –she asked as soon as she entered the room again.

–Perfect! I congratulate you, lady! You have a very smart daughter! A wonderful girl!

My mother looked a little surprised. I don't know why she had to be so surprised with that; It's not that it was so hard to believe…

–Seriously?

–Wonderful! –the doctor kept saying.

XVII.

FINAL SUMMARY

I guess it makes no sense to keep writing about Alina or about Norah, except that they did exist for me. They were my friends, and although it's not something that I say out loud, they still are.

My mother told the whole family about my journal/novel and about the visit to the psychologist.

In response, Granny Trina exposed that the pen was the tongue of the soul, and went on to make a Catalan cream, to celebrate it; meanwhile, Grandma said that I had butterflies in my head, that she had always known, and without saying anything else continued smelling the flowers that she had received from the mailman.

Boni wanted me to let her read what I had written. I was surprised when she said she liked it.

Finally, my father returned from Russia. My mother went to pick him up at the airport. I stayed at home. I was ashamed because she would certainly show him my journal/novel, and I had put him living in the basement.

But my father didn't seem bothered by that. Actually, he seemed very happy and rested.

He arrived and greeted everyone.

—I brought a gift for each one of you! —he announced.

He looked at my grandmother, and stressed:

—For you too, Mariela. And for you, Trina. But let's open them later! Now we go to the beach. It's the last day of summer vacation!

—I'm ready! —I jumped and immediately put on my flowered bikini.

We went to the beach. It was amazing how good it was to be there.

When we got tired of swimming and splashing, I approached my dad. I wanted to be alone with him, to ask him for forgiveness for putting him in a basement in my writing.

–Josefina! –he hugged me. I don't know why; from his mouth my name sounds just perfect–. My little writer! I just have one question.

A question?

–What did the puppy Ps look like?

I smiled. I knew what he was doing.

–Was he from any specific breed?

–No. He was a mutt.

–Good. Because I know where to get a mutt.

–But I don't want a dog anymore. I don't need him now that I have you.

–Of course you're going to have one! You will have a dog today! Come on, let's find him right now!

He got up from the sand. But I held his hand.

–No, not now, Dad. Let's stay at the beach longer.

–Do you want to?

–Yes.

–You too? –he asked my sister and my mother.

They nodded.

–Well, if everyone wants to stay…

–Hee-hee –I laughed.